Blue: Across the Sea

Bysshe Cooper

Published by Bysshe Cooper, 2023.

This is a work of fiction. Similarities to real people, places, or events are entirely coincidental.

BLUE: ACROSS THE SEA

First edition. July 21, 2023.

Copyright © 2023 Bysshe Cooper.

ISBN: 979-8223541462

Written by Bysshe Cooper.

To my friend Vincent, who was always a blessing. If you are reading this, I would not have been here without you.

Blue: Across the Sea

Cover: A picture of Blue and Bartolo sitting back to back next to the ocean on a rocky shore.

Acknowledgement: To my Friend Vincent, who was always a blessing.

Page 1:

Panel 1: A full-width bird's eye view of a hooded figure running through a forest in the night.

Panel 2: A close up of the hooded figure's head. Any facial features are concealed by hood.

Panel 3: A close up of the figure's feet as he's running. They are covered in silver fur and have claw-like nails.

Page 2:

Panel 1: An inset of his right foot getting caught on a rock.

Panel 2: A Bird's eye view of him falling onto the ground.

SFX: Thud!

Panel 3: The hooded figure perks his head up.

Man Offscreen: He went over here!

Man Offscreen: Get the monster!

Panel 4: The figure removes his hood. He has the appearance of a humanoid fox or wolf with silvery fur. He has slight cuts and bruises on his face. He's in his mid-teens.

Panel 5: A bunch of villagers appear out of the woods. They have beards, brown pants, and white shirts. They are carrying axes and spears.

Panel 6: A close up of one of the men's angry faces.

Man: There he is! Get him!

Page 3:

Panel 1: He has a look of terror on his face.

Panel 2: The villagers are charging towards him.

Panel 3: He covers his eyes with his forearm, prepared for the worst.

Panel 4: Nothing happens, causing him to open his eyes.

Hooded Figure: Huh?

Page 4:

Panel 1: A full-page panel of a tall, slender teenager who is standing with his back towards the hooded figure. He has a red leather jacket and baggy, black sweatpants. He has pale skin and shaggy, black hair that reaches his jaw. He is holding a gray machete in his hand. The villagers are gone.

Hooded Figure:...

Page 5:

Panel 1: A full width panel of the teen turning his head to the hooded figure.

Teen: It's okay. They're gone.

Panel 2: A headshot of the hooded figure looking confused.

Hooded Figure:...

Panel 3: A headshot of the teen smiling at him.

Teen: I'm Bartolo by the way.

Panel 4: A full-width of Bartolo grabbing the hooded figure's arm to pull him up.

Hooded Figure: I am Blue.

Page 6:

Panel 1: A full-width panel of the two of them are sitting next to each other by a murky lake.

Bartolo: You're from Farkas? That island's the home of the cynocephali.

Blue: Does it surprise you that I'm from there?

Bartolo: What surprises me is how you came this far by yourself.

Blue: The society is in bad shape. I was a street orphan caught in a dead-end situation. I sailed to this island to find work, only to find they despise us cynocephali.

Panel 2: Blue looks in Low's direction.

Blue: What of you? You don't look like you're from this island, so what brings you here?

Panel 3: Bartolo looks back at him and smirks.

Bartolo: I am an algae gatherer.

Page 7:

Panel 1: A full-width of him pulling a small glass container out of his jacket.

Bartolo: Observe.

Panel 2: A full-width of him leaning down and putting the container into the length.

Blue: What are you doing?

Panel 3: A full-width close up of Bartolo scooping up glowing white algae into his containers.

Bartolo: There are many types of algae among the islands. There are fire, earth, ice, and wind algae just to name a few basic ones. These can be used as fuels for weapons or vehicles, and pretty decent ones at that, but they need someone to collect it.

Panel 4: A full-width of Bartolo holding the container of glowing algae in front of him.

Bartolo: That is where I come in.

Page 8:

Panel 1: A full-width of Bartolo looks away from the container and away from the container and at Blue.

Bartolo: It is a job that pays a lot...

Panel 2: A standard panel of Blue's ears perking up.

Bartolo: ...but it is a lonely one.

Panel 3: A standard panel that's a close-up of Bartolo's algae container.

Bartolo: I have to constantly travel to find algae. I can call people by phone, but I have no one to call. I move around too fast to make connections.

Panel 4: A standard panel of Bartolo looking at Blue.

Bartolo: I could use a travel partner.

Page 9:

Panel 1: A standard panel of Blue looking back at Bartolo, confused.

Blue: We just met. What makes you think I would be good or at least at this?

Panel 2: A standard panel of Bartolo smirking back at him.

Bartolo: Multiple reasons, really.

Panel 3: A full-width of Bartolo explaining to Blue. Bartolo is counting the reasons on his fingers.

Bartolo: You're a cynocephali, a species legendary for their sense of smell, which would definitely come in handy. You sailed here all the way from Farkas, and you're only ten years old. You're a natural-born sailor. And, you don't really have any possessions, so nothing you need to leave behind.

Panel 4: A standard panel of Blue looking back at Barolo.

Blue: Okay, I could be a good algae gatherer. However, that is not the occupation that I wish to pursue.

Panel 5: Bartolo looks concerned back at him.

Bartolo: What is it you want to be, then?

Page 10:

Panel 1: A full-width of Blue whispering into Bartolo's ear. He's listening intently.

Panel 2: A standard of Bartolo's face beaming a surprised expression.

Bartolo: Oh...

Panel 3: A panel of Bartolo looking back at Blue.

Bartolo: We could also be that, too...

Panel 4: A full-width of the silhouettes of Blue and Bartolo looking up at the full moon.

Bartolo: ...one day.

Page 11:

Panel 1: A full-width of the front of a restaurant in a western-style town. There is a dessert surrounding.

Caption: Six years later.

Panel 2: A standard panel of a silhouette wearing a cowboy hat standing in front of the restaurant.

Panel 3: A standard panel of the silhouette walking toward the restaurant from the side. The wind is blowing wildly.

Panel 4: A standard panel that is a close-up of the man's hand pushing the front door open.

Page 12:

Panel 1: A full-page panel of a young man in cowboy attire bursting through the door, holding a gun in his right hand. His face is full of anger.

Cowboy: Okay, everyone on the floor. This is a robbery. Comply and no one will have any holes.

Panel 2: An inset of the customers and a waiter are getting on the ground.

Panel 3: An inset of the cowboy looking to the side.

Man off Screen: Careful where you point that thing.

Page 13:

Panel 1: An inset of a fireball flying through the air.

Panel 2: A full-width of the fireball hitting the gun, causing the cowboy's hand to burn as he drops it.

Cowboy: GGGAAAAHHH!

Panel 3: A standard panel of Bartolo standing in the corner. He is concealed by shadows.

Bartolo: Tsk, tsk, tsk. What a wuss. If you think I am trouble...

Panel 4: A standard panel of him stepping out of the shadows. He looks older, as he is now twenty-two years old. He is wearing yellow pants, a blue shirt, a red leather jacket, and a red handkerchief around his neck. He is wielding a Chinese miao dao sword.

Bartolo: ...Just wait till you meet my partner.

Page 14:

Panel 1: A standard of the cowboy looking confused at him.

Cowboy: Partner? I don't see no partner.

Panel 2: A standard panel of him having a wide-eyed look of pain.

Cowboy: AAAHHHH!!!!

Panel 3: A full-width of the cowboy getting poked in the back by Blue, who is wielding a Bolognese sidesword. Ice is forming around his torso. Blue also looks different, because he is now sixteen. He is still pretty slender. He is wearing blue harem pants, blue suspenders, and a white shirt. He is also wearing circular glasses and has a shaggy mop of hair.

Cowboy: What! I'm freezing. What is this stuff? How is this possible?!

Panel 4: A standard panel of Blue stepping back and pushing up his glasses. He has a know-it-all look on his face.

Blue: It's a thing called ice algae. It's very useful when using it in conjunction with weapons.

Panel 5: A standard panel of Bartolo walking over to Blue.

Bartolo: And that's a wrap.

Page 15:

Panel 1: A full-width panel of them sitting on a bench together. Their swords are at their waists. Bartolo is counting some money in his hand.

Bartolo: That guy managed to fetch a pretty penny now that we turned him in. Bounty hunting is a good side hustle.

Blue: And these algae-powered weapons proved useful. Say, is there enough money to put into the savings account?

Bartolo: Don't worry. We have enough money to buy a boat. We just have to find one to buy before we can become privateers.

Panel 2: A standard of Blue looking at him awkwardly.

Blue: So, are we going somewhere to buy a ship?

Panel 3: Bartolo looks back at him and smirks.

Bartolo: Sure thing. We're heading off to that famed ship-building island you told me about: Berlusia.

Page 16:

Panel 1: A full-width of town filled with buildings made of sand-colored stone. There are streets made of the same material. There are fields of grass in between the buildings and roads. Worried people are running around, carrying baskets of food or money. Men are wearing ponchos and women are wearing silk dresses.

Caption: Meanwhile...

Man: Hurry! It is almost time. They could be here any moment now.

Man: I've heard he's been in a bad mood lately. I believe that.

Panel 2: A panel of someone sitting a basket full of cash at their doorstep.

Woman: This is all we could afford. I hope he takes this.

Panel 3: A standard panel of a man setting a basket of bread at his doorstep.m

Man: Be thankful you could at least afford to give Don money.

Panel 4: A full width of a man watching this from the distance. He is a fairly tall and broad person. He is wearing gray knicker-boxers, a white shirt, and a dark blue vest. He is in his teens and has short, brown hair.

Page 17:

Panel 1: A full-width of Blue and Bartolo getting off a sailboat at the harbor.

Caption: Berlusia.

Blue: I am just saying, do not you ever get tired of staying in motels and needing to take ferries constantly. I just want a place to call our own.

Bartolo: You're right, you're right. I just want to be careful. This is something we'll be living on for a long time. I want to make sure we pick the right one.

Panel 2: A standard of Blue and Bartolo looking off into the distance.

Bartolo: Well, that's odd, don't you think?

Panel 3: A standard of them looking down the street and seeing that there are no people here.

Blue: Where are all the shipwrights Berlusia is famous for? In fact, where is everyone?

Bartolo: Must be a holiday of some sort or something.

Panel 4: Blue and Bartolo are walking down the street.

Bartolo: Would you look at that, a neighborhood. We could probably come here and ask for directions.

Blue: I do not know. Something does not seem right.

Panel 5: A worm's eyes view of Bartolo looking down at something and smiling.

Bartolo: Hey, look at this!

Page 18:

Panel 1: Bartolo is holding a fruit basket. Blue is looking at it skeptically.

Bartolo: How thoughtful of these people. They're leaving food for travelers like us.

Blue: Are you sure? This seems strange.

Panel 2: Bartolo takes a bite into the apple and raises an eyebrow at Blue.

Bartolo: Come on, you need to relax at times. All work and no play makes you a dull boy.

Panel 3: A full-width of Bartolo handing him a pack of uncooked noodles.

Bartolo: Why else would a touristy island like this keep baskets of food on their front porches. There's dragon fruit, Javanese bananas, plums, and even pasta: your favorite.

Panel 4: Blue has a reluctant look on his face as he takes the pasta from him.

Blue: Fine. What else could it be?

Panel 5: Blue and Bartolo have surprised looks as someone yells at them.

Man off screen: What are you two foam heads doing?! Do you want to get killed in some of the most violent ways possible?!

Page 19:

Panel 1: A full-width. Blue and Bartolo look across the street to see that teen in the blue vest from earlier.

Teen: Don't you know what Don Garrito does to those who defy him, no less take what he claims belongs to him!!

Bartolo: What is he talking about?

Panel 2: A full-width of the teen running past them.

Teen: I tried to warn you, so there's no blood on my hands. I'm getting out of here before they come by.

Bartolo: Seriously, what are you talking about!

Panel 4: They look back to see three silhouettes approaching them.

Blue: I think that's who.

Silhouette in the middle: Your friend is right. You should be scared.

Panel 5: The figures stand in front of them. There are two burly guys and a girl with a brunette ponytail dressed like a secretary in the middle.

Secretary: You're new here, so we'll let you off easy. Give us all that's on you and your kneecaps will stay intact.

Page 20:

Panel 1: A full-width of the secretary lady getting punched in the face by Bartolo casually.

Panel 2: A panel of her falling to the ground. Those two guys looked concerned.

Those two guys: Mrs. Osbourne!

Panel 3: Those two guys draw swords at Bartolo. He stands there casually.

Man 1: You're gonna bleed for that!

Panel 4: A full-width panel of Blue knocking the swords out of their hands with his own.

Blue: Great, just great. It always has to resort to the drawing of the blade doesn't it?

Page 21:

Panel 1: A full-width of Blue and Bartolo have their swords drawn out and pointed at those two guys. Blue has a casual look and Bartolo is smirking.

Bartolo: Now, will you tell us what is going on, or will things have to get messy?

Panel 2: A panel of those two guys running off, carrying Ms. Osbourne.

Man 1: Run! It's a cynocephali.

Man 2: I thought those things were just a myth.

Panel 3: Bartolo looks annoyed at Blue.

Bartolo: Hey, I did things in the fight too, didn't I.

Blue: Well, you were the one that recklessly started it.

Bartolo: It was gonna happen, regardless.

Panel 4: They are surprised to hear someone talk to them.

Man off screen: Wow, you took them down without even needing to make much of an effort. That's impressive.

Panel 5: Nice turn their heads to see it's that teen from earlier. He looks excited.

Teen: It's been so long since we have seen anyone so brave around here, let alone two people. And... are those algin weapons? I never thought I'd see them in the hands of fellow civilians? So many things are happening at once!!

Page 22:

Panel 1: A standard panel of Bartolo looking annoyed at him and Blue looking at him confused.

Bartolo: Those are all yes. What is it all to you?

Blue: (What is it with this man? Was not he just calling us "foam heads" a moment ago?)

Bartolo: And I don't mean to be rude, but we are on a tight schedule, so could you keep your answer quick.

Panel 2: The teen is holding his hands up and smiling.

Teen: I do not wish to trouble you, but the answer is pretty complex. Would you two care to join me for dinner?

Panel 3: An inset of Blue and Bartolo looking at each other awkwardly.

Panel 4: A full-width of them smiling at the teen.

Bartolo: Sure thing. I was exaggerating the fact that we are on a tight schedule. It's been forever since we've had a home-cooked meal.

Blue: I would like that very much. Erm... If I could request, I would not like any meat. It causes my stomach to get irritated. I hope that wouldn't be too much...

Panel 5: A full-width headshot of the teen.

Teen: Waldo. My name is Waldo. It won't be much of a problem. We haven't had much meat around here ever since something significant happened in this town.

Page 23:

Panel 1: A full-width of them sitting together at a table on a deck of a large, blue ship. They are eating soup.

Bartolo: Do you really live here?

Waldo: Yes. It is quite common for people here to live on their boats.

Blue: I have read about that.

Panel 2: A full-width of them talking at the table.

Waldo: Really. I heard cynocephali were incapable of reading human languages.

Blue: And I heard humans believe everything they read.

Bartolo: Seriously, though. Blue here is a genius when it comes to geography. That is how he knew to come here. We are looking to buy a boat, and we came here because of the famous shipwrights.

Panel 3: Waldo has a sorry look on his face.

Waldo: I am sorry, but you won't find those here anymore.

Blue: Why is that?

Panel 4: A close up of Waldo's face expressing concern.

Waldo: Don Garrito.

Page 24:

Panel 1: A standard of Waldo explaining to them.

Waldo: It has been almost ten years since then. We were originally a peaceful and economically successful island. That was until he came

Panel 2: A standard of a flashback of Berlusia years ago. It looks the same, only cleaner.

Waldo: It started off just like any other day. None of us were expecting what was going to happen.

Panel 3: A full-width of several, war-like ships approaching the shore.

Waldo: Several ships came out of nowhere and arrived at our shore. There were large amounts of men who were heavily armed, and they were here to make a point.

Panel 4: Several men step out, carrying swords and rifles.

Waldo: They were not subtle. They said that the city was under new leadership. We attempted vainly to stop them.

Panel 5: Several citizens are being held at gunpoint.

Waldo: We tried to fight them off, but they had more weapons than we did, not to mention a few algin weapons.

Page 25:

Panel 1: A picture of a man in a white suit, leather shoes, and a golden necklace. He is sitting on a throne and his face is obscured by shadows.

Waldo: Their leader was a man named Don Garrito. Not much is known about him, no matter how much we tried. There are no records of where he is from or when he was born. It is as if he had literally appeared out of nowhere.

Panel 2: A picture of a scared family huddling in the corner of their house.

Waldo: He was not just satisfied with being our leader, though. He wanted to get rich doing so, and Garrito had just the way to do it.

Panel 3: A panel of three villagers carrying off straw baskets.

Waldo: Once a week, every household is to sit a picnic basket outside on their front porch. It is to be filled with money, food, anything of value.

Page 26:

Panel 1: A full-width of them sitting at the table together, their meals are finished.

Bartolo: I am guessing that today was that day.

Waldo: Indeed. That woman was a collector and those two were enforcers. His force is pretty strong, but he is cautious.

Blue: Cautious about what?

Panel 2: An inset of Waldo's face.

Waldo: Algin weapons.

Panel 3: A full-width of Blue and Bartolo's swords laying on the table.

Waldo: Ever since he took over, he has banned ownership of algin weapons. Having bribed local law enforcement, we are the only ones who can defeat him. He did that to keep us weak.

Panel 4: A close up of Bartolo's face. His eyes are somewhat closed because he is tired.

Bartolo: We got these from a local merchant. They were used, but still in good shape. These weapons have served us well over the last few years.

Panel 5: A close-up of Blue's face looking somewhat cheery.

Blue: Indeed. Algin weapons are designed to last a long time. Some say they could serve a warrior for the rest of their life.

Panel 6: A panel of Waldo holding up Blue's sword close to his face.

Waldo: Indeed. As an engineer and shipwright, I am fascinated by your blade. Sharp and sturdy, it may be, but there is a confusing detail.

Panel 7: A close-up of Blue's sword. It has the name Drake inscribed on it.

Waldo: Who's Drake?

Blue: It was inscribed on my blade when I first got it. I suppose it was either the name of a previous owner or what the blade was named.

Page 27:

Panel 1: A full-width of the three of them getting off the table. Bartolo and Blue are sheathing their swords.

Waldo: Naming sword?

Blue: Sure. Many warriors name their weapon.

Bartolo: I named mine "Hacker". That is because it is good at slashing.

Panel 2: A standard of them walking off Waldo's boat.

Bartolo: When is the next collection gonna be?

Waldo: The Northeastern region. Why so?

Bartolo: We'll remember to steer clear of it on our way out?

Blue: (That will be useful to know.)

Panel 4: Blue and Bartolo are waving goodbye to Waldo.

Bartolo: Well, thanks for the meal.

Blue: (Pains me to do this)

Blue: We'll hopefully visit this island again sometime.

Panel 5: A shot of a fair-sized mini mansion in the center of the city.

Caption: Meanwhile...

Voice inside the house: Sir, you've gotta believe me.

Page 28:

Panel 1: A full-width of Ms. Osbourne on her knees inside the house. She has a black eye.

Ms. Osbourne: But Don, you have to believe me. We were jumped by a man and a cynocephali. They were carrying weapons, algin weapons! Those are strictly against the law, your law. They are hostile and need to have something done about them.

Panel 2: A diagonal panel of Don Garrito sitting on his throne. His face is still obscured by the shadows.

Don: Hehehehe. Never in my days, Osbourne, never in my days have I seen a cynocephali this far from Farkas, nonetheless one that was carrying algin weapons. To be honest with you, I thought you were going crazy. Then again...

Panel 3: A diagonal that is a close-up of his face. He has tan skin, wavy blonde hair, and a faint mustache.

Don: There's a first time for everything, isn't there?

Page 29:

Panel 1: A standard of Don standing and looking away from Ms. Osbourne.

Don: This is not the first time I have faced opposition. I have overcome a lot more challenging obstacles than this in order to meet my goals.

Panel 2: Don looks back at Ms. Osbourne.

Don: You're a smart one. You should know that cynocephali come from Farkas. They are indeed dangerous, but we are not in Farkas. We are in Berlusia, and in Berlusia, I am in charge.

Panel 3: Don Garrito looks closely at Ms. Osbourne. She looks horrified.

Don: You think of me as incapable of maintaining my leadership, do you?

Ms. Osbourne:...No sir...

Don: I guarantee you, my men under my leadership will have these two out of town by the end of tomorrow.

Panel 4: Don Garrito sits back down on his throne. **Panel 5:** An inset of Don's face looking sarcastic.

Don: (Besides, I was able to handle having a nagging woman as one of my collectors.)

Page 30:

Panel 1: A full-width of Blue and Bartolo are walking across a field.

Blue: It occurs to me, Bartolo: why didn't you talk about our bounty hunting careers to Waldo last night. Your mouth is usually bigger than that.

Bartolo: I figured if one resident Berlusian found out, then others would find out. If the Berlusians find out, Don Garrito will find out. If Don Garrito finds out, we likely won't be able to collect a bounty from him.

Panel 2: A full-width of Blue looking offended at Bartolo.

Blue: Hey, you said we would focus on getting a boat so we could become privateers.

Bartolo: Hey, that was before I knew that there was someone like Don Garrito ruling Berlusia.

Blue: That does not change the fact that you said it.

Panel 3: A standard panel of Bartolo sitting down next to a rock.

Bartolo: Look, my friend, we cannot buy a ship from here with Don Garrito running the place. Berlusia has the best ship-building industry in this time zone, in your own words. I just want nothing other than the best when it comes to our boat.

Panel 4: Blue sits down next to Bartolo.

Blue: Sorry for getting mad, Bartolo. It's just that I was looking forward to just getting a boat and not having to chase some dangerous criminal down.

Panel 5: Blue and Bartolo look over the rock.

Bartolo: Wait a minute! What is that!

Blue: Based on what I learned from Waldo, I think I know what it is.

Page 31:

Panel 1: A splash of a small village down the hill has several stacks of smoke coming from it. Several houses have broken windows.

Bartolo: I reckon I haven't seen anything this destructive in this part of the sea.

Blue: I ponder if Don Garrito has anything to do with this.

Bartolo: Wonder? You wonder? This has to be Don Garrito.

Panel 2: A standard of the two of them running down the hill.

Bartolo: I hope none of the villagers were hurt, or worse yet.

Blue: Knowing who this guy is, I would not wish that you get your hopes up.

Panel 3: A standard of their faces looking despondent.

Blue: Oh dear...

Bartolo: No questioning this time. It has to be Don Garrito.

Blue: That or someone who is a subordinate to him.

Page 32:

Panel 1: A full-width of the village. Several houses have burn marks and broken windows.

Bartolo: I can only imagine what sorts of things happened here.

Blue: Not to speak of what minor thing caused it. Men like him get upset very easy.

Panel 2: A standard of Bartolo picking up an ear of corn that is covered in ash.

Bartolo: I feel for these villagers. They have to work themselves sick just so they could appease some ingrateful scum. It really leaves a bitter taste in my mouth in more ways than one.

Panel 3: Blue perks his left ear up. Bartolo is in the background.

Blue: Wait, wait, wait. Do you hear that?

Bartolo: Hear what?

Blue: There's someone here. He is breathing heavily.

Panel 4: They walk around a corner, trying to find a person.

Bartolo: Hard to believe a living being would choose to stay here after this raid.

Blue: Maybe he couldn't.

Bartolo: You would be surprised what someone would be willing to do. They could limp off if they needed to.

Panel 5: Their faces bear expressions of shock.

Blue:...

Bartolo:...

Page 33:

Panel 1: A standard of Waldo sitting against a wall. He is without his glasses and his face is covered in bruises.

Blue: Waldo?!

Bartolo: Dude! What in the world happened here.

Panel 2: A standard of Waldo looking up with weak eyes.

Waldo: I was in this village doing business. It turns out Don Garrito had declared that there would be another day of collecting in this village. These people gave what they could, but it was apparently not enough.

Panel 3: A full-width of Blue and Bartolo looking at him intently.

Waldo: They became violent, really violent. People, even the children, were in danger. I tried to stop them, but I couldn't. They gave me quite the beating, I would say. They had weapons, they did, but they did not use them. They said that my blood was not good enough to touch their weapons. I might have not been able to stop those men, but it was not necessarily in vain. I was able to distract them long enough for the villagers to escape.

Panel 4: Blue and Bartolo are helping him up.

Bartolo: Good job, Wally. You did all you could.

Blue: And without a weapon, nonetheless.

Waldo: Bartolo...

Panel 5: A standard with Bartolo standing in the center. There is a silhouette behind him of a man with a stick.

Waldo: ...watch out behind you!

Page 34:

Panel 1: A standard panel of an old, short man with a cane flies by in between Blue and Bartolo.

Blue: Woah!

Bartolo: Everyone is crazy these days.

Panel 2: A splash of the old man standing on the ground. He is wearing a white polo shirt and blue shorts. He has a white captain's hat on. He is waving his cane in the air.

Old man: Crazy! Speak for yourselves. You just announce we have to pay taxes with no time in advance and then destroy our town because we couldn't get it in time and then call us crazy! You know what? Just come a bit closer and me and my cane will show you crazy!

Panel 3: Waldo grabs that man.

Waldo: Jose, it's okay. These are the two guys I was telling you about: Blue and Bartolo.

Jose: Huh?

Page 35:

Panel 1: Waldo has one hand on the shoulder of Jose. He is explaining to Blue and Bartolo.

Waldo: Forgive him. This is Jose, he is the mayor of this town.

Jose: You're right, I am.

Waldo: Well, at least he was before Garrito took over. He's always jumpy around the time of collection.

Panel 2: A standard of Bartolo shaking hands with Jose.

Jose: Forgive me for that, Bartolo. I thought you were one of Don Garrito's collectors.

Bartolo: No sweat, sir. I can understand why you act like that after a raid like this one.

Panel 3: Blue, Bartolo, Jose, and Waldo are standing there but are surprised when they hear a voice.

Voice: Grandpa, are they gone yet?

Jose: Juan?

Panel 4: A little kid standing out there in the middle of the road. Everyone is looking at him. He is wearing blue shorts and a red shirt. He has short, black hair. Waldo is pointing to the left.

Juan: Wow! Is that a real cynocephali?

Jose: Juan! You're okay.

Bartolo: Wait, when was this raid?

Waldo: It was just now. They went that way.

Panel 5: Blue is examining Juan.

Blue: These people are fortunate no one got hurt. Right, Bartolo?

Panel 6: Blue looks up to see that Bartolo is gone.

Blue: Bartolo...?

Page 36:

Panel 1: A full-width of Bartolo standing in front of a crowd of burly men. Each one is wielding either a sword or a rifle.

Man: Who is this guy?

Man: This is the same guy that attacked Ms. Osbourne.

Man: You're gonna pay for that, punk!

Panel 2: A close-up of Low putting his hand on his sheathed sword.

Low: You call me a punk...

Panel 3: A close-up of him inserting a container of brown algae into his blade.

Bartolo: ...but you are the ones who did all this.

Panel 4: A full-width of him cutting their weapons in half using his sword.

Bartolo: Earth algae!

Man: Watch out! He's wielding an algae weapon.

Man: Wish the Don could have lent us some.

Page 37:

Panel 1: Bartolo kicks one of the men in the stomach.

Man: Gah!

Panel 2: Bartolo crosses blades with one of the men.

Bartolo: Impressive...

Panel 3: Bartolo punches him in the jaw.

Bartolo: ...but not impressive enough.

Man: Ack!

Panel 4: A silhouette of Bartolo non-lethally cutting a man in the stomach.

Bartolo: Don't worry. This won't hurt me a bit.

Panel 5: He hits another man in the face with the pommel of his sword.

Bartolo: Just kidding. It's nothing but a flesh wound.

Panel 6: Three men behind him point pistols at his head.

Bartolo: Eh?

Man: Stop right where you're standing.

Page 38:

Panel 1: A full-width of an air slash knocking the pistols out of their hands.

Man: What in the sea!

Panel 2: Blue is standing on a hill.

Blue: Bartolo, if you focus more on what's going around than your witty banter, you would not find yourself in these situations.

Man: What was that? Was it due to algae?

Panel 3: Blue is inserting a container into the pommel of his sword.

Blue: No, that was just an advanced technique used in western swordsmanship. This, however, is due to algae.

Panel 4: Blue is holding his sword up in the air and a tornado is coming from it.

Blue: Wind algae!

Panel 5: Blue slings the tornado out at them like a whip. They go flying.

Page 39:

Panel 1: Blue looks confused.

Blue: Something is wrong. This is all too simple.

Panel 2: Several men jump out from behind him, wielding swords and axes.

Man: Get the cynocephali.

Man: Watch out for his sword.

Blue: Oh... it all makes sense now.

Panel 3: Blue spins the wind whip around and knocks the men back.

Panel 4: A man behind Blue tries to hit him in the neck with a sword.

Bartolo: Blue, watch out!

Blue: Seriously...?

Panel 5: Bartolo looks shocked and surprised.

Sfx: Thud!

Page 40:

Panel 1: The man's face looks scared.

Blue: You know...

Panel 2: Blue is revealed to have caught that blade in his mouth.

Blue: You people tend to rely on surprise attacks too much.

Panel 3: Blue elbows him in the ribs, knocking him over.

Blue: Do not be so surprised. You knew I was a cynocephali, did you not?

Page 41:

Panel 1: Blue slides down the hill to meet Bartolo at the bottom.

Bartolo: Nice work you did up there, Blue.

Blue: Do not give me any of that flattery.

Panel 2: Blue points a finger at Bartolo and looks annoyed.

Blue: That was very irresponsible of you. You could have been walking, no, running, straight into a trap for all you knew.

Bartolo: I am aware of that Blue, but these people needed help, and lots of it.

Panel 3: Blue and Bartolo continue to argue.

Blue: I know that, but...

Bartolo: Withhold not good from them to whom it is due, when it is in the power of thine hand to do it.-Proverbs 3:27

Panel 4: Blue looks at Bartolo awkwardly.

Blue:...

Bartolo:...

Panel 5: Blue smiles at Bartolo.

Blue: Okay, you are right.

Bartolo: I'm just following what is.

Blue: We both do.

Bartolo: You're right about that.

Page 42:

Panel 1: A full-width of them sitting at a dinner table inside a hut with Waldo, Jose, and Juan.

Jose: What you two young firecrackers did today was reckless. However, it was also brave.

Juan: Yeah. You chased guys out of town. You simply just cut their weapons up, and then punched one in the face. And Blue the Cynocaephali caught a blade in his mouth. I mean, how cool is that?

Bartolo: I like him. He reminds me of a younger version of myself.

Waldo: Anyway, we meant to tell you this: It was reckless due to the fact that Don Garrito is going to get even angrier.

Panel 2: Blue and Waldo looking at each other.

Blue: Well then, I guess there is no turning back now.

Waldo: You've got that right!

Panel 3: Bartolo is holding a glass of water.

Bartolo: I don't suppose you have any ideas for our next move, Mister Mayor?

Panel 4: Jose is holding a rolled up map.

Jose: It just so happens that Waldo here and I have uncovered something of use.

Page 43:

Panel 1: Waldo and Jose are laying out the map on the table.

Waldo: As the former mayor of the city...

Jose: Current mayor!

Waldo: As mayor of the city, he has a lot of informants.

Panel 2: A bird's-eye view of the map of Berlusia they laid out.

Waldo: As you are already aware, Berlusia is comprised of many ports. These ports have been mainly closed ever since Don Garrito took over. However, some are occasionally used for exporting goods out of the country.

Panel 3: Blue and Bartolo look at Waldo?

Blue: Why is that?

Waldo: What other way is there for Don Garrito to get the money to support both his kingdom and his lavish lifestyle?

Panel 4: Waldo pointing back at the map.

Waldo: Anyway, these "goods" they're exporting are actually all the things we put in the baskets other than the money. Like I said before, they rely on these trades to keep up Don Garrito's empire.

Page 44:

Panel 1: Jose talking to the group.

Jose: Don Garrito has established this system ever since he abolished the shipwright industry around here.

Panel 2: Jose is looking off into the sky. There is a flashback of people building a boat.

Jose: I miss those days. It was a simpler time. People worked for their own money. After Garrito took over, though, he made it where he controlled all the businesses. Instead, we give him all our earnings and he gives us measely living conditions as a return.

Panel 3: Jose looks down with his eyes closed, sad.

Jose: (Sigh) How the times have changed.

Page 45:

Panel 1: Waldo is talking to everyone.

Waldo: Exactly. His economy relies on things like this.

Panel 2: Waldo holds a finger up as he explains.

Waldo: If even one ship were to be stopped, it would create a hole in his systems.

Panel 3: Bartolo looks at Waldo, serious.

Bartolo: I take that it is our job to be the ones who stop it.

Waldo: Correct.

Panel 4: Waldo points back at the map.

Waldo: In light of recent events, we have uncovered the location of where the next ship will be sent.

Panel 5: A close-up of Waldo's face with him putting his two hands together.

Waldo: Here's how it all goes down…

Page 46:

Panel 1: A panel of the map with Waldo pointing to a port on the east end.

Waldo: The port that we are going to be attacking is going to be here.

Panel 2: Waldo draws a circle around the port.

Waldo: There will be many guards here, so we will need to use the cover of darkness to our advantage.

Panel 3: Waldo draws a line from the port he circled to a large building near the top of the map.

Waldo: They are transporting goods from Don Garrito's mansion using this path. We might get spotted by some of his men, so we'll have to stay clear of it.

Bartolo: Wait a minute…

Panel 4: Bartolo looks up at Waldo, confused.

Bartolo: If we know where Don Garrito's mansion is, how come we don't just sneak into there and confront Don Garrito, with the tips of our swords it is.

Page 47:

Panel 1: Jose and Waldo look at Bartolo.

Jose: That would not be a good idea.

Waldo: It sure wouldn't be.

Panel 2: A splash panel of Don Garrito's mansion. It resembles a castle made of sandstone and marble.

Waldo: The building was originally the town meeting hall, which was for important issues. Ever since Don Garrito took over, he decided to make it into his home. It may seem nice and fancy, but don't let it fool you. There are guards at every corner, a testament to how paranoid he is. Each one is armed to the teeth. I would doubt you two could break into there.

Panel 3: Waldo, somewhat annoyed, points back to the map.

Waldo: Now, could we please continue on with the plan.

Page 48:

Panel 1: Juan and Jose are rolling a barrel into the room.

Waldo: It has taken a while, but we have finally gathered up enough explosives in secrecy. This should come in handy. Fortunately, you two have algin weapons. Once this barrel gets close enough to the boat, then you can use fire algae to ignite it from a distance.

Panel 2: Blue and Bartolo get up from the table.

Bartolo: How many men are in on this.

Panel 3: Jose walks up to the table.

Jose: It's just the four of us.

Blue: That doesn't seem ideal.

Waldo: I know it doesn't but you will understand. We do not want Don Garrito getting word of this. The less people we have to trust, the better.

Panel 4: Bartolo leans against the wall.

Bartolo: Okay, then. When does this go down, again?

Waldo: Tonight.

Page 49:

Panel 1: Don Garrito is yelling at one of his henchmen inside the mansion.

Don: What!

Panel 2: He points an accusing finger in the henchman's face.

Don: Are you telling me that a whole horde of men was taken down by only one man and one cynocephali?!

Man: Yes sir, but these were not ordinary people. They were carrying algin weapons.

Don: Tell me something I didn't know!

Panel 3: The man is shrugging.

Man: They caught us by surprise. We didn't know what to expect.

Don: Fine! Just fine!

Panel 4: He turns his back on the man.

Don: You have told me this when I was in good humor, so I'll let you off easy, but I need a favor.

Man: Yes, sir!

Don: Bring me that "Special Package" that came in today.

Man: Yes, sir.

Page 50:

Panel 1: The man runs off as Don looks out the window.

Don: (So hard to find good workers these days)

Panel 2: He starts to grin as he looks out the window.

Don: However, it will all soon pay off.

Panel 3: He examines his watch.

Don: When the time is right, I will accomplish my mission here and then will move on.

Panel 4: He looks up.

Don: Finally.

Panel 5: He sits down.

Don: It is one of those things you hate until you get to the end.

Page 51:

Panel 1: A large full-width panel of the loading dock. The ground is covered with his men, who are wearing black sailor suits.

Panel 2: Two of them are talking to each other. Each are holding a rifle.

Man: Did you hear what they are saying?

Man: Yeah. Do they really think that he's a cynocephali?

Man: I know. What is one doing all the way from Far-

Panel 3: Each of them are whacked in the back of the head with a stick.

Man: Gah!

Man: Ugh!

Panel 4: Jose stands by the heads of the unconscious men.

Jose: Don't be so upset. That is more than you deserve. Are you ready Waldo?

Page 52:

Panel 1: Waldo appears out of the corner.

Waldo: W-Why wouldn't I be?

Panel 2: Waldo and Jose are dragging those two behind a wall.

Jose: You seem nervous.

Waldo: You think I'm nervous! I am nervous! Do you know what will happen if we get caught?

Jose: Not so loud.

Panel 3: They are there with those men and Blue and Bartolo behind that wall.

Bartolo: Do this quickly, before they realize these two are gone.

Blue: And we still have an opening.

Panel 4: The opposite side of the wall

Bartolo: Quickly, get it on.

Blue: It is a little baggy.

Bartolo: Who cares? Just put it on.

Page 53:

Panel 1: Blue and Bartolo walk out from behind the wall, rolling the barrel of explosives.

Blue: Will they not notice that I am a cynocephali?

Bartolo: Just keep your hat down and cover your face.

Blue: Okay.

Panel 2: They roll the barrel past some of the soldiers, who are playing cards.

Bartolo: It is late at night, and I feel like that it has taken a toll on these people.

Blue: (Why is always so confident about me doing things like this.)

Panel 3: They stop in front of the boat. Blue is pointing to the front of the hull.

Bartolo: Where do you think we should put this thing?

Blue: The front of the hull there should cause it to sink.

Bartolo: You sure? We don't have any chances to test that.

Panel 4: Blue puts his hand on his face as he's thinking.

Blue: I am visualizing this in my head and I cannot see what would go -

Panel 5: A spotlight shines on Blue and Bartolo.

Man: It's them. That's the man and cynocephali that Don Garrito is after.

Bartolo: Looks like we have less time than we thought.

Page 54:

Panel 1: Bartolo kicks the barrel, sending it rolling.

Blue: What are you doing?

Bartolo: Putting it in position.

Panel 2: Bartolo draws his sword.

Bartolo: Ignite it when it gets close. Me and Hacker will hold them off.

Panel 3: Bartolo loads a canister of algae into his sword.

Bartolo: Quickly! I can only hold them off for so long.

Blue: I am on it.

Bartolo: Wind algae!

Panel 4: A wind beams from Bartolo's sword.

Bartolo: I'll think of what comes next when we get there.

Page 55:

Panel 1: The barrel stops right next to the ship. Blue draws his sword.

Blue: Now would be the right time to use Drake.

Panel 2: Blue shoots a stream of fire from his sword at the barrel.

Blue: Fire algae!

Panel 3: The barrel exploding. Blue is pumping his fist.

Blue: Yes! I got it. That ship is as good as sunk!

Panel 4: The fog clears to reveal that there is a dent in the ship, but not a crack. Blue's face is shocked.

Blue: What! It is still floating?!

Page 56:

Panel 1: Waldo and Jose are looking over the wall together, shocked.

Jose: Are ya kidding me?! It only left a dent.

Waldo: It seems I have made a slight miscalculation!

Panel 2: Bartolo, still fighting them off with wind algae, looks back.

Bartolo: Sink this! What are we going to do now?!

Panel 3: Blue and Bartolo are looking at each other.

Blue: Do you still have any wind algae, Bartolo?

Bartolo: Yeah. Why?

Panel 4: Blue is loading a canister of algae into his sword.

Blue: I just made a new plan.

Panel 5: Blue points his sword toward the dent.

Blue: Can you fly me up there?

Page 57:

Panel 1: Bartolo uses the wind to fly towards Blue.

Bartolo: And you say I'm the one with crazy ideas.

Panel 2: Bartolo grabs Blue as he flies by.

Bartolo: What now?

Blue: This.

Panel 3: A large-width of Blue stabbing the indentation of the ship.

Blue: Earth algae!

Page 58:

Panel 1: Blue rips open a large tear in the side of the ship.

Bartolo: You tore a hole in the ship!

Blue: Now we just let the water do the work.

Panel 2: Jose and Waldo are watching the ship sink. Jose looks joyous. Waldo looks stunned but relieved.

Jose: I knew those two could do it.

Waldo: Y-Yeah. I guess I should have seen that coming.

Panel 3: Don Garrito's men are watching the ship sink in terror.

Man: Don Garrito is not going to be happy!

Man: You think?! His trade system has just been messed up.

Panel 4: The ship is almost completely sunk.

Man: It's going to take him a long time to make up for this loss.

Man: You mean it's going to take us a long time.

Page 59:

Panel 1: The soldiers look at each other.

Man: It is because of those two! Where are they?

Man: That is what I intend to find out. Spread out and find them!

Panel 2: Underwater, you can see Blue and Bartolo swimming off away from the ship.

Bartolo: (That was one close call.)

Blue: (I know Don Garrito is more than a little unhappy right now.)

Panel 3: They swim close to shore.

Bartolo: In all my days as a bounty hunter, I have never experienced a mission this crazy.

Panel 4: They wash up on shore.

Bartolo: Can we just sit here and appreciate the fact that we survived.

Blue: I am too shocked that worked to appreciate it.

Page 60:

Panel 1: Jose and Waldo ran up to them.

Waldo: That was crazy, guys.

Jose: I still can't wrap my head over this.

Panel 2: Jose helps Blue up and Waldo helps Bartolo up.

Bartolo: What can we say, this is what we do.

Blue: Though it has never gotten this crazy.

Panel 3: Jose looks concerned at them.

Jose: Are you two okay?

Bartolo: We're fine, by some crazy chance.

Panel 4: Blue looks up at Jose and Waldo.

Blue: There is still one part that confuses me.

Waldo: What is that?

Panel 5: A close-up of Blue's face.

Blue: How did that spotlight find us all of a sudden in the middle of the crowd.

Page 61:

Panel 1: Blue and Bartolo are sleeping in a room. Blue is in the bead. Bartolo is on the couch.

Bartolo: That is a good point you had there, Blue.

Panel 2: A panel of Bartolo sitting up.

Bartolo: How come they just happened to find use when we were surrounded in a vulnerable position instead of out in the open.

Panel 3: Blue looks back at Bartolo.

Blue: I know it might just seem like a coincidence, but my years with you have taught me never to overlook things. This is just not something that cannot be ignored.

Panel 4: Bartolo lays back down.

Bartolo: Then again, it could just be a coincidence.

Page 62:

Panel 1: A standard of Blue laying back down.

Blue: I suppose it could be that. However, it would have been one severely unfortunate coincidence.

Panel 2: A close up of Bartolo closing his eyes.

Bartolo: That's what I like about you, Blue.

Panel 3: A full-width of the room with Blue and Bartolo going to sleep.

Bartolo: You never overlook anything, not once in the six years we've been together can I remember you overlooking anything.

Page 63:

Panel 1: It is a bright and sunny day. A panel that is a close-up of the sun.

Panel 2: A young child is walking on the sidewalks. He is wearing brown pants and a red shirt. He has a brown buzz-cut and bright skin. The buildings and streets look abnormally clean and neat.

Child: My, what a wonderful day it is. It is not every day it is this sunny but not scorching hot.

Panel 3: He looks over his shoulder and hears someone coming.

SFX: Step, Step, Step

Child: Who could that be?

Panel 4: A round man steps around the corner. He has green pants, a white shirt, a rope belt, and a bandanna around his head. He has bright skin and a large, brown mustache.

Man: Kid. There you are! What are you doing? Going on a stroll like this, when there are repairs we need to work on today?

Panel 5: The child looks back at the man.

Child: Is that today, Johann?

Page 64:

Panel 1: A standard of Johann looking up while standing in front of the child.

Johann: What in the world caused you to forget that?

Panel 2: A full-page splash of Johann looking up at the sun.

Johann: Well...It seems to be a nice day, doesn't it? Now I see why.

Panel 3: Johann gets on one knee and places a hand on his child.

Johann: I'll make you a deal. We'll go on a good stroll. Okay?

Child: Okay.

Page 65:

Panel 1: A full-width of a large, blue ship at the yard.

Caption: it's just another day when it comes to working.

Panel 2: Johann is tying a rope on the ship while the child is watching.

Johann: This is how you tie the rigging to the timbers. Are you paying attention?

Child: Yes, sir.

Johann: Don't talk like that to me. It makes me feel old.

Panel 3: Johann motions to a bucket of soap.

Johann: Alright, you have had your lesson for today. Now you must scrub the deck.

Panel 4: The child is carrying the bucket of soap and a mop off.

Child: You don't have to remind me. I am on it, Johann.

Page 66:

Panel 1: The child is scrubbing the floor.

Child: Not that I am complaining. I am quite okay with this job.

Panel 2: Johann is on the deck, fixing a loose floor board.

Johann: It is good that you are thankful. Remember Psalms 118:24.

Panel 3: Johann stands back up.

Johann: It will bring you a long ways, trust me.

Panel 4: Johann and the child look at each other.

Johann: Well, that is all for today. You are beginning to be a good shipwright, kid.

Panel 5: The kid is looking up at Johann.

Child: Really?

Page 67:

Panel 1: A standard panel of Johann and the child walking down the street.

Johann: We don't get every day like this, do we?

Child: We do not.

Panel 2: They sit down on a bench.

Johann: So, you want to be a shipwright?

Child: I've been your apprentice for almost a year now. You know I do.

Panel 3: A full-width of them looking at each other.

Johann: Why do you want to become a shipwright?

Child: I don't know. It is just something I'm good at. Why did you become a shipwright, Johann?

Panel 4: A full-width of the two of them looking into the sun.

Johann: To help people.

Child: What do you mean?

Page 68:

Panel 1: Johann and the child look at a tree.

Johann: You see, life is short.

Child: Uh huh.

Johann: It's just that there are important things in this life.

Panel 2: Johann looks down at the child.

Johann: I don't want my life to be wasted. I wish to do something significant. Something that will help people, for years to come.

Panel 3: Johann points at himself.

Johann: That is why I became a shipwright.

Page 69:

Panel 1: A picture of a ship sailing across the sea.

Caption: "There are several uses of ships. Many things rely on them."

Panel 2: A side-view of a ship carrying crates.

Caption: "First of all, our economy relies on these boats for transport. Sure, there are planes these days, but they can't carry as much. Without these boats, our economy would struggle."

Panel 3: A picture of people handing crates with medical symbols to villagers.

Caption: "Just look at all the people who need medicine out there. How do you think all the medicine gets there? By ships like these, nonetheless.

Panel 4: A panel of a ship sailing towards an island.

Caption: To sum that all up, look at all the missionaries using boats.

Page 70:

Panel 1: A panel of Johann looking at the child.

Johann: It is a humble life, kid, but nonetheless one that is needed.

Panel 2: Johann gets up from the bench.

Johann: Do you see what I mean?

Child: Yes, I do.

Panel 3: The child looks up at Johann.

Child: Johann...Thank you?

Johann: For what?

Panel 4: The child hugs Johann.

Child: For showing me why I want to be a shipwright.

Johann: What do you mean?

Panel 5: A close-up of the child's smiling face.

Child: It is the same as yours.

Page 71:

Panel 1: Johann looking down at the kid.

Johann: (That kid is going to do great things one day.)

Panel 2: The man and the kid are shocked when they hear a loud noise.

SFX: Bang!

Johann: What could that be?

Child: I don't know.

Panel 3: They are even more shocked. Johann grabs the child.

SFX: Bang! Bang! Bang!

Johann: I'm starting to get worried.

Panel 4: Johann stuffs the child in a trash can.

Child: What are you doing?

Johann: Getting you to safety!

Panel 5: Johann pulls out a pistol. The child peaks out from the trash can.

Child: What's going on?

Johann: I have no idea, but I'm ready for what it is.

Panel 6: Johann, looks down at the trash can.

Johann: Stay safe so more people can.

Panel 7: Johann runs off.

Child: What do you mean?

Page 72:

Panel 1: An inset of Waldo's eyes opening.

Panel 2: Waldo almost jumps out of bed from the bad dream he had.

Waldo: Johann!

Panel 3: Waldo rubs his face.

Waldo: It's just a dream...It's just a dream...It's just a dream.

Panel 4: Waldo slams his head back on the pillow.

Waldo: Who am I kidding? It's not a dream. It's a memory.

Page 73:

Panel 1: A full-width of Blue and Bartolo eating Breakfast with Jose. Bartolo has a banana, Blue has pancakes, Jose has a glass of juice.

Jose: Do you two boys feel fine?

Bartolo: Sure thing. You'd be surprised what a good night's sleep will do to a person.

Panel 2: Blue is cutting his pancakes with a knife.

Blue: When do we make our next move?

Panel 3: Bartolo looks up at him.

Jose: The best thing to do would be to wait for Don Garrito's next move.

Bartolo: Good call.

Page 74:

Panel 1: Blue wipes his mouth with a napkin.

Blue: Patience is a virtue in war. It's Just like in chess, go, or life in general.

Panel 2: Jose takes a drink of his juice. Bartolo nods in agreement.

Bartolo: When fighting a larger threat, one should wait for an opening.

Jose: Uh huh.

Panel 3: Bartolo looks at Jose.

Bartolo: Any more leaks from your informants.

Jose: Waldo is the one you should be asking that.

Panel 5: Blue and Bartolo look surprised.

Bartolo: Hey, wait a minute. Where is Waldo?

Jose: He's busy running errands.

Page 75:

Panel 1: Bartolo looks down, relaxed.

Bartolo: Well, it looks like we will just have to-

Panel 2: Waldo bursts through the door, surprising everyone.

Bartolo: -wait.

Panel 3: Waldo places his hands on the table and is panting wildly.

Blue: Waldo, are you doing well?

Waldo: No...

Jose: What is wrong with you, boy?

Panel 4: Waldo sits down.

Waldo: I was in the market, buying our groceries. That was when I came across one of our informants. H-He said he wanted to speak with me.

Panel 5: A close-up of Blue's concerned face.

Waldo: He s-said that he was l-looking for me. I asked him if there was a more private place, but he said that this was something that needed to be done here and now.

Panel 6: A close-up of Bartolo's concerned face.

Waldo: He said that Don Garrito was mad about how mad his shipments were not making as much money as they used to.

Panel 7: A close-up of Jose's concerned face.

Waldo: Don Garrito said that there was still one way to make the money he needs.

Page 76:

Panel 1: A full-width of Waldo explaining. Everyone bears almost cartoonish expressions of shock.

Waldo: Don Garrito is going to destroy the village.

Bartolo, Blue, and Jose: What!

Panel 2: Blue stares at Waldo intensely.

Blue: Waldo, please explain what you mean.

Waldo: I mean what I said.

Panel 3: Low and Jose stare at each other, thinking.

Waldo: Don Garrito is going to tear apart the village and take as much as he can. Then, he is going to set sail and conquer another village.

Panel 4: Bartolo looks down.

Bartolo: That does it!

Page 77:

Panel 1: Bartolo looks back up.

Bartolo: We make our next move now.

Panel 2: Blue leans across the table towards Bartolo.

Blue: What exactly do you suppose we do?

Bartolo: When is this raid, again?

Panel 3: Waldo's head pops up.

Waldo: I don't know exactly, but I know that is soon.

Panel 4: Bartolo looks at everyone.

Bartolo: Then we will go after him today.

Waldo: What?!

Page 78:

Panel 1: Blue puts his hand on his chin as he thinks.

Blue: Actually, that makes sense. It uses the same logic as when we sunk the raid.

Panel 2: Jose looks at Blue.

Jose: What do you mean?

Blue: Think about it, we were able to catch his men off-guard because they were busy.

Panel 3: Bartolo stands up.

Bartolo: Exactly. They will be busy preparing for the departure. There will be less people to guard Don Garrito's mansion.

Jose: Why does it have to be so soon, though?

Panel 4: Bartolo takes a drink of water.

Bartolo: People will get hurt, or worse, during this raid. I don't want to postpone our response and be too late. It's worth the risk.

Panel 5: Blue stands up.

Blue: Bartolo is right!

Bartolo: What else is new?

Blue: If we wait too long, there won't be a second chance.

Page 79:

Panel 1: Jose tips his head down, thinking.

Jose: Okay, but how are you two going to get in?

Panel 2: Bartolo places his hand on his sword.

Bartolo: You leave that up to us.

Waldo: What are you two going to do when you get there?

Panel 3: Blue stands next to Bartolo, who places his hand on Blue's shoulder.

Blue: That is simple. We will take him hostage and force him to surrender.

Bartolo: Then we will turn him in for a hefty bounty.

Page 80:

Panel 1: A scene inside Don Garrito's mansion. He is sitting on his throne with a man standing next to him.

Caption: Inside Don Garrito's mansion...

Don: Don't water the message down. Tell how the evacuation is going.

Panel 2: A panel of the man looking at a notebook as he talks to Don Garrito.

Man: We have completely cleared out the northern portion of this house. We are still working on all the others. At the moment, we are about halfway done clearing out the house.

Panel 3: Don gets up from his throne casually.

Don: That is fine enough, servant. Carry on with what you are doing.

Panel 4: Don Garrito is standing by the window.

Man: Sir, are you sure that there is nothing you want us to do?

Don: I'm too busy to work on the fine details of everything.

Panel 5: A close-up of Don Garrito's smirk.

Don: I have bigger things to worry about.

Page 81

Panel 1: A panel of a security camera on the wall.

Panel 2: A panel of the security camera getting frozen in ice.

SFX: BUZZ!

Panel 3: A panel of Blue and Bartolo walking along the wall, which is covered in frozen security cameras.

Bartolo: That's the last one.

Blue: For now, at least.

Panel 4: A worm's eye of Blue and Bartolo looking at their swords. A cold steam flows off of them.

Bartolo: Waldo was right. Even without guards, there still are a lot of security cameras.

Blue: It was fortunate that we chose to pack algae.

Panel 5: They walk around a corner.

Blue: Have you seen anyone, Bartolo?

Bartolo: No. why?

Page 82:

Panel 1: They walk past a barrel.

Blue: I know that Don Garrito's men are busy with the evacuation, but you don't think he would leave any of them to protect his mansion?

Panel 2: They walk around another corner.

Bartolo: I guess Don Garrito just made a bad move. I normally would be skeptical as well, but we should take advantage of this.

Panel 3: They walk down a hallway.

Blue: Don Garrito may be annoying, but he is not stupid.

Page 83:

Panel 1: They stand by a door at the end of the hall.

Bartolo: He probably no longer cares about this mansion, since he is leaving.

Panel 2: They enter the large room.

Bartolo: See, there is no one here. Everyone must be loading everythings.

Panel 3: Blue's right ear perks up.

Blue: Wait a minute. Do you hear that?

Bartolo: Hear what?

Panel 4: Suddenly, there is a bright yellow flash. You can see Blue and Bartolo's silhouettes.

Blue: Ow!

Bartolo: W-What just happened?

Caption: "All personnel, to the gymnasion.

Page 84:

Panel 1: A splash. They open their eyes to see that they are surrounded by Don Garrito's men.

Bartolo: Would you look at that? You were right.

Panel 2: A silhouette of Don Garrito in the crowd walks closer to them.

Don: Well, well, well...so you are the two that have been showing me how incompetent my men are. I must ask...

Panel 3: He steps forward, smirking wide.

Don:...what is a cynocephali doing all the way from Farkas?

Page 85:

Panel 1: Blue has a defensive look on his face.

Blue: That is none of your concern!

Bartolo: So you're Don Garrito!

Panel 2: Don Garrito fakes flattery with one hand on his chest.

Don: I am indeed. You're not as dumb as you look.

Bartolo: If we were so dumb, then why were we able to take down your men.

Panel 3: Don Garrito rolls his eyes.

Don: Oh please. Anyone can take on a grunt! You couldn't even dream of outsmarting me.

Panel 4: A silhouette steps up next to Don Garrito.

Don: You couldn't even match up to my right-hand.

Page 86:

Panel 1: Blue and Bartolo look mortified.

Bartolo:...

Blue: ...Waldo...

Panel 2: Waldo walks up next to Don Garrito. His head is down and he is holding a large blunderbuss-like gun.

Don: Indeed! For years now he has been holding the coveted position of my right-hand man. He did not accept it at first, but everyone had their price. Hahahaha.

Panel 3: He rests his arm on Waldo's shoulder.

Waldo: He was the one responsible for the flash you just experienced. You see, this strange gun is an algae-powered weapon. He used a subtype if algae called...

Panel 5: Bartolo looks up, with a stern look on his face.

Bartolo: Flash algae. It is a subtype of fire algae that grows in regions far south of here.

Don: Well, you seem to be an algae gatherer indeed. Waldo's information is actually quite good.

Page 87:

Panel 1: Don Garrito snaps his fingers.

Don: If you really are an algae gatherer, then you'll find this amusing. Fetch me my armament!

SFX: Snap!

Panel 2: Two men carry a heavy box to him.

Don: As you know, algae can be used to make powerful weapons. If you know the right people, you can get your hands on the weapons you need.

Panel 3: An inset of Don reaching into the box.

Don: Just as in all aspects of my life, I have taste in what weapons I use.

Panel 4: He pulls out a large, gray bazooka.

Don: We do not have very many of these. However, thanks to Waldo here, we are able to maintain them.

Panel 5: Don Garrito slings the bazooka onto his back. Waldo looks shocked.

Don: Just wait till I get to use this on the town. My heart leaps at the thought of getting in on the action.

Page 88:

Panel 1: A full-width Waldo has a shocked expression on his face.

Waldo: What are you talking about?! You said that there was not really going to be a raid on the kingdom of Berlusia! You said it was just bait!

Don: So what? I just made a last-minute change to fit our current situation.

Panel 2: Don rubs his chin while he looks at Blue and Bartolo.

Don: Don't worry. I'm not going to kill you. I recognize good men when I see them. We could always use two good algae gatherers for our weapons.

Panel 3: Blue and Bartolo look back at him, angrily.

Bartolo: And you say we're the dumb ones. We would never work for someone like you.

Blue: After all you have tried to do to us, and you think we are going to work for you. You are nothing short of demented. Not to mention anything you have done to the people here.

Panel 4: Don Garrito looks back at them angrily.

Don: Well, if you're gonna be so ignorant...

Panel 5: Don Garrito looks surprised as the end of Waldo's gun pointed at his head.

Don:...Uhhh...

Page 89:

Panel 1: A full-width of an angry Waldo pointing his gun at Don Garrito's head.

Waldo: Just! Shut! Your! Mouth!

Don: Waldo? What is the meaning of-

Waldo: I said shut your mouth! I cannot stand anymore of your lies! You may think they have grown mundane to me, but you are wrong. DEAD WRONG!

Panel 2: A close-up of Waldo's angry face.

Waldo: I remember life before you came here, Don Garrito! It was great and pleasant, and I long for those days to come back! I joined you because you promised not to enslave or hurt anyone!

Panel 3: A close-up of Don Garrito's face.

Waldo: Don't you dare ruin my name by telling people I joined out of my own will!

Panel 4: A panel of a spear being held to Waldo's throat.

Waldo: Huh?

Voice off-screen: That's enough of that.

Page 90:

Panel 1: A full-width of two large men wearing white suites and short haircuts. One has a spear and one has a large ax.

Waldo: Encio?! Marcion?!

Caption: Encio and Marcion-Don Garrito's two best fighters.

Panel 2: Don Garrito steps behind Encio and Marcion.

Don: Do you really think I would reveal myself without my bodyguards here?

Panel 3: Don Garrito smugly rubs his hair back.

Don: Your attempts at preventing this raid are pathetic. To be honest, we could not pull off this raid if it was not for the element of surprise. These villagers are cowards. We may have the better weapons, but they have the better numbers. They would absolutely demolish us if they tried, but they're all just too scared to.

Page 91:

Panel 1: Waldo holds his head down.

Waldo: Don Garrito...

Panel 2: Waldo smiles as he pulls his vest back to reveal a microphone. Don Garrito has a cartoonish face fault.

Waldo:...For revealing that through the P.A. system in the mansion.
Don: WWWHHHAAAAAAAT!
Panel 3: A crowd gathers outside Don Garrito's mansion.
Man: Did you hear that?!
Man: They're planning to raid the village?!
Panel 4: A close-up of Jose standing in the crowd.
Jose: Ya know, why am I not surprised by this.
Page 92:
Panel 1: A full-width of Don Garrito holding Waldo by the shirt collar.
Don: Why you...! After all this time...!
Panel 2: A full-width of Blue and Bartolo surrounded by guards. Their attention is turned to Don and Waldo.
Blue: Hey, now's our chance.
Bartolo: You're right. We have a distraction on our hands.
Blue: Time for the winter storm.
Panel 3: A close-up of Blue and Bartolo placing their hands on their sheathed swords.
Bartolo: Wind algae!
Blue: Ice algae!
Panel 5: Don Garrito looks back.
Don: What in the world?!
Page 93:
Panel 1: A splash of a winter storm blowing the guards away. Blue and Bartolo have their swords raised in the air.
Blue and Bartolo: Winter Storm!
Panel 2: Waldo gets knocked against a wall.
Waldo: Ow!
Panel 3: Don Garrito gets knocked against a wall next to the exit.
Don: UGH!
Page 94:
Panel 1: Don Garrito gets back on his feet.

Don: How could this get worse?!

Panel 2: Don Garrito runs out the exit.

Don: I never thought I'd have to resort to damage control in a place like this.

Panel 3: Waldo runs after Don Garrito.

Waldo: Don't let him get away!

Panel 4: Blue and Bartolo run to the door.

Bartolo: Do you think we can trust him?

Blue: I have not the faintest idea, but what other choice do we have?!

Page 95:

Panel 1: A full-width of Marcion and Encio, brandishing their weapons, jump in front of the exit.

Encio: You did not think things would be that easy, did you.

Bartolo: One side! We've sunk the others, so save yourselves the pain.

Marcion: Those were just the grunts. We're his personal fighters.

Panel 2: Blue and Bartolo hold their swords in fancy fencing stances.

Blue: Looks as though we have to trust Waldo to take care of Don Garrito while we humble these brutes.

Panel 3: Marcion tries to smash them with his axe, but they jump inside.

Marcion: Less talking!

Panel 4: Encio tries to stab Blue, but he blocks it with his sword.

Encio: How come I get the runt!

Blue: Hey!

Panel 5: Blue elbows Encio in the face.

Encio: Ah!

Page 96:

Panel 1: Encio falls onto the floor.

Blue: I will have you know, I am a standard height for a cynocephali my age.

Panel 2: The tip of Encio spear lights on fire.

Encio: Wolf, cynocephali, dog: None of it changes anything.

Panel 3: A fireball shoots out of his spear at Blue.

Encio: Fire algae!

Panel 4: Blue blocks it with his sword.

Blue: Ice algae!

Panel 5: A large cloud of steam surrounds them.

Blue: That was a bad idea.

Panel 6: The cloud clears and Encio is behind Blue.

Encio: You bet it was!

Page 97:

Panel 1: Bartolo steps back to avoid a horizontal swing from Marcion.

SFX: Swish!

Panel 2: Bartolo steps back to avoid another slash.

Marcion: Won't you stay still for just one minute?!

Bartolo: Lazy much?

Panel 3: Bartolo falls backward, evading a downward strike from Marcion.

Marcion: I'll show you lazy! Earth algae!

Panel 4: On one knee, Bartolo blocks a strike from Marcion with Hacker.

Bartolo: (He's right. These guys are tougher that the others.)

Page 98:

Panel 1: A close-up of the tip of Encion's spear being thrusted.

Encio: I'm done playing around.

Panel 2: Blue spins around and blocks his spear.

Blue: As am I. I shall counter your punte with the most dreaded riposte.

Encio: Huh?

Panel 3: A close-up of Blue's face.

Blue: Fencing terms. By the way...

Panel 4: He scratches Encio's torso.

Blue: Being a cynocephali does make a difference.

Page 99:

Panel 1: A splash of Waldo running through the halls with his blunderbuss.

Waldo: Show yourself, Garrito!

Panel 2: He stops and looks around.

Waldo: Your plan has already failed. Things will be a lot easier if you surrender.

Panel 3: Don Garrito peaks round the corner with his bazooka.

Don: That is what you think!

Page 100:

Panel 1: A full width of Don firing an ice blast from his bazooka. Waldo tries to dive out of the way.

Don: Ice algae!

Panel 2: A small glacier forms, freezing Waldo's lower body.

Waldo: That got me by surprise!

Panel 3: Don Garrito walks by Waldo.

Waldo: Believe me. I would love to finish this now, but there is somewhere I need to be.

Panel 4: Don Garrito runs away.

Waldo: You mean running away from the angry mob!

Don: Zip it!

Page 101:

Panel 1: Blue tries to cut Encio, but he blocks it with his sword.

SFX: CLANG!

Panel 2: Encio jumps back.

Encio: I'll admit, you're tougher than you look, but let's see how you handle this.

Panel 3: Encio delivers a fast blur of thrusts toward Blue with his spear, which now has a brown tip.

Encio: Earth algae!

Panel 4: Blue sidesteps the thrusts and flanks Encio.

Blue: Even if your attacks are strong enough to move mountains, they're useless if they don't hit your opponent.

Panel 5: Blue's sword, Drake turns on fire.

Blue: Let me now show you how to properly use fire algae.

Panel 6: They cross weapons.

SFX: CLANG!

Panel 7: Encio drops his weapon and shakes his hand like crazy.

Encio: GAH! That burns!

Page 102:

Panel 1: Bartolo swats away Marcion's ax with his sword.

Bartolo: Okay, now I'm getting annoyed!

Panel 2: Bartolo kicks him in the stomach with his right leg.

Panel 3: Bartolo kicks him in the stomach with his left leg.

Panel 4: Marcion grips his stomach.

Marcion: What are you doing?

Bartolo: Fighting dirty.

Marcion: That's not how you're supposed to fight!

Page 103:

Panel 1: Bartolo shoves the container into the handle of Hacker.

Bartolo: What are the use of rules in no-holds-barred situations? You do what you have to.

Panel 2: He points his sword forward.

Bartolo: Observe.

Panel 3: He delivers a compressed air slash, but Marcion ducks and dodges it.

SFX: Swish!

Panel 4: Marcion lifts his ax up and prepares to strike.

Marcion: Bad move using air algae.

Page 104:

Panel 1: A splash of Marcion getting frozen in ice.

Marcion: W-W-What just happened?! Y-You just loaded it with wind algae. How'd y-you cover me in i-i-ice?!

Panel 2: Bartolo nods his head as he sheaths his sword.

Bartolo: I never used wind algae. I just simply used an advanced fencing technique that allows me to project slashes using compressed air.

Panel 3: He turns around and walks away.

Bartolo: I knew you wouldn't know what it was, so it set me up for a surprise attack.

Page 105:

Panel 1: A splash of Blue and Bartolo walking away from the defeat of Encio and Marcion.

Bartolo: I never knew that it would work.

Blue: That is the thing with new ideas. You cannot know for sure if they work until you try them.

Bartolo: Now that that's over with, we only have one matter of business left.

Panel 2: A close-up of Blue's face.

Blue: Let us get Don Garrito.

Page 106:

Panel 1: They run down the hall.

Blue: This is where Waldo chased after Don Garrito.

Panel 2: They stop in front of a little glacier.

Blue: Looks like someone used ice algae.

Bartolo: The only weapon that could do this is Don Garrito's bazooka.

Blue: So he was here.

Panel 3: They walk around the glacier to find Waldo, whose feet are frozen.

Waldo: Good to see that you guys are okay.

Blue: What happened here?

Waldo: No time to explain! He went over there!

Panel 4: Bartolo takes out his sword.

Bartolo: Shouldn't we free you first.

Waldo: NO! NO! NO! This ice is thawing quickly. I'll be free soon! It's Don Garrito you need to go after.

Panel 5: Blue and Bartolo run off.

Blue: Sure thing, Waldo!

Bartolo: Stay safe!

Waldo: (Wow. They agreed to that without a fight.)

Page 107:

Panel 1: Don Garrito, carrying his bazooka, runs down the hall with his men.

Don: We should still be able to take the escape ship! It's just down the...

Panel 2: Don Garrito opens the door to the outside but has a shocked expression on his face.

Don:...street.

Panel 3: A full-width of the crowd of people surrounding the back of Don Garrito's mansion. They are yelling and wielding shovels and mallets.

Don: Where did all these people come from?!

Page 108:

Panel 1: Don looks back, seeing Blue and Bartolo behind him.

Blue: These are all the people you have been so cruel to all these years.

Bartolo: It's time to pay the piper, Garrito.

Panel 2: Don Garrito steps nervously back and points his bazooka at them.

Don: Stay back or I'll fire.

Panel 3: Blue and Bartolo look angry as they step forward.

Bartolo: Come on! That's just a bluff!

Blue: You would harm yourself firing it at this distance...

Panel 4: A close-up of Don Garrito's sweaty brow.

Blue:...and you would not want that, would you?

Page 109:

Panel 1: Blue and Bartolo are shocked as they hear a voice behind them.

Voice: Not so fast!

Bartolo: Oh no.

Panel 2: Blue and Bartolo turn around to see Ms. Osbourne and Juan. She is holding a knife to Juan's throat.

Bartolo: Not you again!

Ms. Osbourne: Zip it or else!

Panel 3: Don Garrito regains his relaxed complexion and stands up straight.

Don: Many thanks, Ms. Osbourne. I knew I could rely on you. Now...

Panel 4: A close-up of Blue and Bartolo's angry but concerned faces.

Don: Now, who is it going to be: Me or him?

Panel 110:

Panel 1: A full-width of Waldo whacking Ms. Osbourne with the butt of his rifle. Juan runs away.

Waldo: I think they would like both!

Ms. Osbourne: GAH!

Panel 2: Blue and Bartolo smirk as they look at him.

Bartolo: Waldo! Looks like that ice thawed quickly.

Blue: Speaking of thaw, I know just what to do with Don Garrito.

Panel 3: Blue turns around and fires a beam of fire.

Blue: Fire algae!

Panel 111:

Panel 1: The beam of fire hits Don Garrito's bazooka.

Don: WHAT!

Panel 2: Don Garrito drops the Bazooka and shakes his hand wildly.

Don: GAH! That miserable brat!

Panel 3: Steam begins fuming from his bazooka. Don Garrito looks terrified.

Don: What is going on?!

Man: It's gonna blow!

Panel 4: Blue, Bartolo, and Waldo get on the ground.

Bartolo: EVERYONE HIT THE DIRT!

Page 112:

Panel 1: A full-page splash of a large explosion.

SFX: KABOOM!

Panel 2: A standard panel of Blue and Bartolo covering their faces.

Panel 3: A standard of Waldo covering his face.

Panel 4: A standard of Jose and the people in the crowd covering their faces.

Page 113:

Panel 1: A full-width of a large soot mark on the ground where Don Garrito and his men were standing. They are gone without a trace. The wind blows some of the soot.

Panel 2: One of the men in the crowd looks shocked and confused.

Man: Is he... Is he gone?

Panel 3: Blue and Bartolo look confused but stern.

Blue: ...

Bartolo: ...

Panel 4: Bartolo breaks out a smirk and closed eyes.

Bartolo: Well, isn't this a time for celebration.

Page 114:

Panel 1: A full-width of the Berlusian streets crowded with people celebrating.

Panel 2: A full-width of a group of men and women playing lutes, dulcimers, and accordions for the celebration joyfully.

Panel 3: Two men pass out blue and gray balloons and churros to children.

Panel 4: A panel of Ms. Osbourne and some of Don Garrito's men in stocks and have tomatoes thrown at them.

Page 115:

Panel 1: A full-width of Jose and Juan among the crowd of people throwing tomatoes at them.

Juan: This is great, Grandpa!

Jose: Enjoy it, Juan. This is a time of great celebration.

Panel 2: A close-up of Jose's smiling face.

Jose: And to think, we owe all this to two youngsters who I tried to whack with my cane. Heehee!

Panel 3: Juan looks up at Jose.

Juan: Where are they, by the way.

Panel 4: Jose picks up another tomato.

Jose: They are just taking a break from the festival.

Panel 5: He throws the tomato at Ms. Osbourne.

Jose: They have unfinished business.

Jose: Bullseye!

Page 116:

Panel 1: Blue, Bartolo, and Waldo walk through a forest.

Blue: You said there was a ship you found eligible.

Bartolo: Couldn't this have waited. I still haven't gotten to try the churros.

Waldo: Yes guys, there is a ship and we will be able to go back to the festival. There is just something I want you to see.

Panel 2: They walk up next to a headstone shaped like a cross in the forest.

Panel 3: Waldo reaches into his coat pocket.

Blue: Is that Johann's grave?

Waldo: Yes. It is.

Panel 4: Waldo places a bundle of yellow flowers on the grave.

Waldo: I never saw him again after that raid. I built this, so I would never forget him, not that I ever could.

Panel 5: Bartolo places his hand on Waldo's shoulder.

Bartolo: He would be glad to see what a good guy you've become.

Waldo: Thank you, Bartolo.

Panel 6: They walk off.

Waldo: Now I can show you what I wanted to.

Panel 117:

Panel 1: A full-width of them walking out of the woods and onto a beach.

Waldo: Here we are.

Bartolo: Huh?

Panel 2: Blue and Bartolo look surprised as Waldo smiles and crosses his arms.

Bartolo: This ship seems familiar.

Blue: Is this not the ship that you live in, Waldo?

Panel 3: Blue, Bartolo, and Waldo look at his Blue ship.

Waldo: It sure is.

Bartolo: Of all the ships you could sell, why are you selling us the one you live on.

Waldo: Things are changing around here because of you two. This is just a little thing compared to all that's happening.

Panel 4: Blue and Waldo look at each other.

Blue: What is the price you want for it?

Waldo: It's unconventional.

Panel 118:

Panel 1: A close-up of Waldo's smiling face.

Waldo: Take me to sea with you.

Panel 2: Waldo is explaining to Blue and Bartolo.

Waldo: When I helped you two overthrow Don Garrito, I felt such a sense of joy overcome me. Fighting for something bigger than yourself, that's what I want to do, as a privateer. It's just like what Johann said to me.

Panel 3: A flashback of Johann talking to Waldo.

Johann: Stay safe so more people can.

Panel 4: Blue and Bartolo look at each other, smiling.

Bartolo: After all we've been through together, you know the answer is yes.

Blue: Besides, we could use a shipwright.

Panel 5: Waldo shakes hands with them.

Blue: It is settled, then. We set sail by the end of the week.

Page 119:

Panel 1: Bartolo places his hand on the hull on the ship.

Bartolo: All we need now is a name for the ship.

Panel 2: Blue scratches his chin and smiles as he thinks.

Blue: I have an idea. How about...

Panel 3: A splash of Waldo, Bartolo, and Blue smiling, happy with the name.

Blue:...The Nautic Johann!

Page 120:

Panel 1: A full-width of a sloop sailing across the ocean.

SFX: Meanwhile...

Don Garrito: I can't believe this!

Panel 2: He sits on a lawn chair on deck. He is covered with many bandages.

Don: Because of two meddling drifters and my own right-hand, years of hard work is thrown away.

Panel 3: The ship sails off.

Don: When did my life become this crazy?

Page 121:

Panel 1: A panel of a hand with a white glove holding a steaming cup of tea.

Voice: Hmm...

Panel 2: A full-splash of a figure wearing a wide-brim hat and a black trench coat and slacks. No features on his face are shown due to a shadow cast over his face by the hat. He sits on the rocky shores.

Man:...Very interesting.

Attention!

If you, the reader, are willing and able to illustrate this script, please contact

bysshe.cooper@gmail.com.

I prefer a sharp, stylistic, black-and-white style.

Thank you.